P9-DJL-597

EMILY'S MAGIC WORDS

Emily Post

Please, Thank You, and More

By Cindy Post Senning, Ed.D., and Peggy Post

Illustrated by Leo Landry

Collins

An Imprint of HarperCollinsPublishers

For Casey, Jeep, Dan, and Will
—P.P. and C.P.S.

For Mary and Sophie
—L.L.

Collins is an imprint of HarperCollins Publishers.

Emily's Magic Words: Please, Thank You, and More
Text copyright © 2007 by Cindy Post Senning and Peggy Post
Illustrations copyright © 2007 by Leo Landry
Manufactured in China.
Library of Congress Cataloging-in-Publication Data
Senning, Cindy Post.
   Emily's magic words: pleasae, thank you, and more / by Cindy Post Senning and Peggy Post;
illustrated by Leo Landry. — 1st ed.
      p.   cm.
   ISBN-10: 0-06-111680-7 (trade bdg.) — ISBN-13: 978-0-06-111680-3 (trade bdg.)
   ISBN-10: 0-06-111681-5 (lib. bdg.) — ISBN-13: 978-0-06-111681-0 (lib. bdg.)
   1. Etiquette for children and teenagers. I. Senning, Cindy Post. II. Landry, Leo. III. Title.
BJ1857.C5P67 2007   2006019582
395.1'22—dc22   CIP
                                                                                                            AC

Typography by Jeanne L. Hogle
1 2 3 4 5 6 7 8 9 10
❖
First Edition

EMILY'S MAGIC WORDS

Emily can do magic.
Do you know how?

With words!

Magic words!

PLEASE

THANK YOU

GOOD-BYE

HELLO

EXCUSE ME

What makes these
words magic?

Well, they can open doors . . .

please have a cookie.

. . . and make smiles appear.

Thank you.

These words can make friends . . .

Hello, Jerome!

Hi, Grandma!

How are you, Nutmeg?

even if they disappear from time to time.

"See you soon, Jerome!

Bye, Grandma!

So long, Nutmeg!

These words can turn a frown into a smile . . .

. . . or fix a mistake.

Now that you know Emily's magic words,

you can do magic too!

There are three more magic words.

They are the most magical of all.

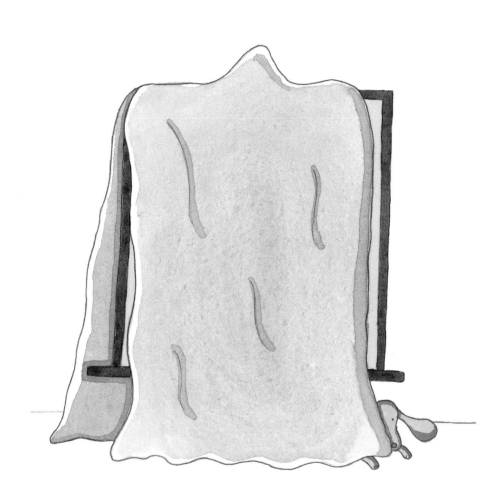

Do you know what they are?

Of course you do!

⌐★ Note to Parents

ETIQUETTE IS MORE THAN JUST MANNERS AND MAGIC. It is also about three fundamental principles: respect, consideration, and honesty. Even though your toddler is too young to seriously grasp these principles, if you teach basic manners now, you'll be building a climate that reflects respect, consideration, and honesty . . . and magic!

Teaching manners to toddlers can be challenging. They are bundles of energy, curiosity, and unrestrained joy in their widening worlds. They are also beginning to acquire basic social skills—using magic words and table manners, sharing, and taking turns. These are the underpinnings of etiquette and good manners. By helping your toddlers acquire these skills, you are helping them build a firm foundation for all the manners still to come.

There are two basic strategies that should guide you as you teach manners to any child regardless of age:

1. Know what to expect, and then expect it. Take the time to learn what your child is capable of developmentally. Then expect neither too much nor too little!

2. The Golden Rule of Parenting—always behave the way you want your children to behave.

Your children will learn the most from watching you. If you tell them to do one thing and then you do another, they will do what you do, not what you say. Respect them, show them what consideration is, and be honest in the kindest of ways. Then the manners you teach will be meaningful and will last a lifetime.